ORSON

SHELDON

BOOKER

ROY

WADE

D0124643

W9-AEX-905

All the animals squeezed into Santa's sleigh, including Wade, who was afraid to fly and had to cover his eyes. Santa gave a whistle, and his reindeer whisked them up into the frosty air.

For the animals of U.S. Acres, it was the merriest, most magical Christmas of all. And even Roy had to admit that Orson's Christmas contest was a pretty smart idea!

Then Santa turned to Sheldon. "Are you ready to ride in my sleigh?" he said.

"I'd love to!" said Sheldon. "But . . ."

"But what?" said Santa.

"It just wouldn't feel like Christmas without all my friends."

"Then bring them along!" said Santa.

"Hurray for Sheldon!" cried the animals.

". . . Sheldon!"

Sheldon! The animals were amazed.

"But Sheldon didn't even enter the contest!" complained Lanolin.

"Sheldon showed the true spirit of Christmas by helping each and every one of you," said Santa. "Giving is what Christmas is all about."

"You've all worked very hard," said Santa. "And you've all shown a lot of Christmas spirit. But one of you has discovered the true spirit of Christmas. I declare that the winner of The Great Christmas Contest is . . ."

In rushed Roy, wrapped up like a big Christmas present.
"Look at me, Santa!" he said. "I'm the biggest Christmas present ever! That's more spirit than anyone else!"

"But Roy, I thought you said this contest was a dumb idea," said Santa.

"Just kidding, just kidding," said Roy, grinning nervously.

When Santa told Bo that his drawing was beautiful, Bo gave him a big hug!

"I'm very glad your story has a happy ending," Santa said to Orson. "And now I suppose you'd like me to choose a winner."

"Wait! Wait!" someone cried.

Santa admired Blue's wreath and said Lanolin's stocking
was one of the nicest he'd ever seen.

"You make a beautiful Christmas tree," he told Wade.
"I hope these lights don't singe my feathers," said Wade.

Santa tasted Booker's cookies. "These are even more delicious than minced worm pie!" he said.

Next Cody barked Christmas carols for Santa. Santa applauded loudly at the end.

It was the real Santa Claus!

"You came to judge our Christmas contest!" cried Orson.
"Of course," said Santa. "After all, spreading the Christmas
spirit is what I do best."

"And carry a sack full of corn," added Wade.
"And wear an old red sweater," said Blue.
"And have a beard made from my wool!"
cried Bo.
"Where's the real Santa Claus?" demanded
Lanolin. "I'll bet he isn't coming at all!"
"Ho, Ho, Ho! Merry Christmas!" said a jolly voice.

The animals stared.
"What's going on here?" asked Lanolin.
"Don't you recognize Santa?" Orson replied.
"You're the goofiest Santa *I've* ever seen," said Booker.
"Since when does Santa have a curly tail?" complained Cody.

Orson hid in the hayloft until the disappointed animals returned. Then he jumped out and shouted, "Ho, Ho, Ho! Ho, Ho, Ho!" Unfortunately, he was too busy ho-ho-hoing to watch where he was going!

FOOMP

Orson fell out of the loft into a big pile of hay!

While the other animals ran outside to look, Orson ran to his trunk. Quickly he put on an old red sweater, a red and white ski cap, and a beard he had made from leftover sheep's wool. He threw a beat-up feed sack over his shoulder.

Later that night all the animals except Roy
gathered in the barn to wait for Santa Claus.
At first they were full of Christmas cheer. But
then they became restless.

"We want Santa Claus! We want Santa
Claus!" they shouted.

"Do I hear sleigh bells?" said Orson.

Christmas Eve had finally arrived, and Orson was starting to panic. Santa hadn't replied to his letter. Maybe Roy was right about Santa Claus!

There was only one thing to do. "If Santa Claus can't judge our contest," said Orson, "then Santa Pig will do it!"

"Do you have any more great ideas?" groaned Wade.

"Maybe you should just hang an ornament from your bill," said Sheldon.

"That sounds a lot safer to me."

Wade carefully placed an orna-
ment on the end of a branch.
The tree quivered.
And then . . .

. . . all the snow leaped
from the branches and
buried poor Wade!

FOOMP

Wade took a box of decorations from
the barn, and he and Sheldon hiked into
the woods. Before too long they came
upon a tall, snow-covered fir tree.

"This looks perfect," said Sheldon.
"Okay, Wade, start decorating."

"I'm worried."

"Christmas trees can't hurt you," said
Sheldon.

Wade couldn't even think about the contest. He was
afraid his ideas were no good!

"Here's an idea," said Sheldon. "Why don't you find the
most beautiful Christmas tree in the woods and decorate it?"

"I'm afraid I'd get lost in the woods."

"I'll go along," said Sheldon.

Orson decided to write a Christmas story about a pig who invents a Christmas contest that's supposed to be judged by Santa Claus.

I hope this story has a happy ending, thought Orson.

Cody practiced barking Christmas carols.

Blue made a beautiful wreath out of pine branches and ribbon.

Bo thought his crayon drawing of an angel would surely win the Christmas contest.

"Hold still, Sheldon," said Bo. "I'm almost finished."

"Good," said Sheldon. "I'm getting tired."

Lanolin decided to show her Christmas spirit by knitting
a Christmas stocking.
"Isn't your stocking a bit large?" asked Sheldon.
"The bigger the stocking, the bigger the presents," said Lanolin.

What a busy and exciting week it was for everyone!
Everyone except Roy, who woke the animals each morning
by blowing his bugle and shouting, "This is still the
dumbest idea I've ever heard!"

The two wet chickens went home to warm up by the stove.

"M-m-m-maybe I should just b-b-b-bake Christmas cookies," said Booker, his teeth chattering.

"S-s-s-sounds good t-t-t-to me," said Sheldon.

"Come closer, boys," said the worm. "My elf will take your picture with old Santa."

"That's a funny camera," said Sheldon.

"Smile," said the elf worm.

"AAAAAARGH!" cried Booker, soaking wet. "I'm gonna pound you worms!"

"Merry Christmas!" called the worms, safe under ground.

Booker and Sheldon walked along, looking for worm tracks.
"There's a worm!" shouted Booker. "Let's pound him!"
"You wouldn't pound Santa Claus, would you?" said the worm.
Booker stopped. "But you're just a worm."
"Ho, Ho, Ho," said the worm.
"He does sound like Santa Claus," said Sheldon.

Just then Booker came along. "Have you decided what to do for the contest?" he asked.

"Not really," replied Sheldon. "How about you?"

"I'm going to bake a special Christmas treat. It's called minced worm pie."

"I'll help," said Sheldon.

Not far away, on a little hill behind the barn, Sheldon was doing some serious thinking. I'd really love to ride in Santa's sleigh, he thought, but it's hard to show your Christmas spirit when you're just an egg with feet.

Dear Santa,
I know
bus...

Orson decided he'd better try to reach Santa right away.
"I know you're busy on Christmas Eve," Orson wrote.
"But I'd appreciate it if you could come to U.S. Acres
to judge our Christmas contest. Please let me know.
Your friend, Orson.

"P.S.," he added. "Would you ever let someone ride
in your sleigh?"

"Aren't you going to enter the contest, Roy?" said Orson.

"Why should I?" Roy answered. "It's bound to flop. Because you know there's no Santa Claus."

"Of course there is," said Orson.

Roy laughed. "I can't wait till Christmas Eve. You are going to be in BIG trouble."

"Stop it!" said Orson. "That's no way to show Christmas spirit!"

"We'll show you Christmas spirit," said Lanolin. "You just make sure that Santa is here on Christmas Eve."

"He'll be here," said Orson. "I promise."

Booker, Sheldon, Bo, Lanolin, Wade, Cody, and Blue started planning for the contest. Roy stomped off to the chicken coop, with Orson on his tail.

Everyone was very excited, except Roy.

"This is the dumbest idea I've ever heard, Orson," said Roy.

"Well, I think it's a great idea," replied Lanolin.

"Fuzzface!" yelled Roy.

"Bugbreath!" shouted Lanolin.

"What do you get if you win?" asked Lanolin.

Orson hadn't thought about that! "Uh, the winner gets to ride in Santa's sleigh . . . "

"Wow!" said the animals.

" . . . because Santa himself will be here to judge the contest on Christmas Eve!"

"Hey, everybody!" cried Orson.
"Have you heard about The Great
Christmas Contest?"

Booker stopped chasing worms.
"The Great Christmas Contest?" he said.
"What's that?"

"It's a contest to see who can show the
most Christmas spirit," said Orson.

Orson thought very hard about how he could bring the
Christmas spirit to U.S. Acres.

Doesn't anyone here know that Christmas is coming? Orson
asked himself. We need some Christmas spirit right away!
Orson dove into his waller to think about this problem.

Unfortunately, the waller was frozen! FOOMP! Orson hit
the hard mud and slid into a snowbank!
"I hate winter wallers," he moaned.

Orson poked his head through the barnyard fence and frowned. Christmas was just a week away, but he was the only one at U.S. Acres who seemed to care!

In the barnyard, everyone was carrying on as usual! Booker chased a worm. His brother, Sheldon, listened to music. Lanolin splattered Roy with snowballs. Blue tried to keep Cody from scaring Wade, which wasn't easy, because Wade was afraid of *everything*! And Lanolin's twin brother, Bo, hugged a snowman.

Jim Davis

THE
GREAT CHRISTMAS
CONTEST

from the creator of GARFIELD®

Written by Jim Kraft

Illustrated by Paws, Inc.

BANTAM BOOKS
TORONTO • NEW YORK • LONDON • SYDNEY • AUCKLAND

Copyright © 1988 United Feature Syndicate, Inc. All rights reserved. Published by
Bantam Books, a division of Bantam Doubleday Dell Publishing Group, Inc.
Published simultaneously in the United States and Canada. Printed in the United
States of America. ISBN 0-553-05807-X

THIS
BOOK

BELONGS
TO

Taylor & Lauren Rector